I AM READING

CAPTAIN PEPPER'S PETS

SALLY GRINDLEY

Illustrated ˡ

DAVID PA

KINGFISHER

To Chris and Richard Downs – S.G.

To the staff and children of
St. Faith's Infant School, Lincoln – D.P.

KINGFISHER

First published 2002 by Kingfisher
This edition first published 2004 by Kingfisher
an imprint of Macmillan Children's Books
a division of Macmillan Publishers Limited
20 New Wharf Road, London N1 9RR
Basingstoke and Oxford
Associated companies throughout the world
www.panmacmillan.com

ISBN: 978-0-7534-1469-9

Text copyright © Sally Grindley 2002
Illustrations copyright © David Parkins 2002

The moral right of the author and illustrator has been asserted.

2 4 6 8 10 9 7 5 3 1
1TR/0808/WKT/FR/115SM

A CIP catalogue record for this book is available from the British Library.

Printed in China

Contents

Chapter One

Captain Pepper wanted a pet –
but he didn't want a parrot.
"Every pirate I've ever
met has had a parrot,"
he said.
"Parrots talk too
much. No, I want
a pet that will
make me famous
all over the world."

"So let's go to the pet shop," said Pirate Nong.

"Goldfish are best," said Pirate Noodle.

"Let's buy a hamster!" said Pirate Noddypoll.

"Daft twits!" roared Captain Pepper. "A hamster or a goldfish won't make me famous! What I want is something different."

What Captain Pepper wanted Captain Pepper got.

So off they sailed, aboard the *Snooty Fox*, to search for a pet that was different.

Chapter Two

The pirates sailed for many long

weeks.

At last, they reached an island.

"Ah-ha!" cried

Captain Pepper.

"I'll bet my

boots we'll find

my pet here.

Full speed ahead,

you horrible lot!"

They sailed down a river and into
a jungle.

"Stop!" bellowed the Captain.

"Lower the gangplank and get ashore!
Find me a pet, or I'll feed you to the
sharks!"

Then Captain Pepper lay down
in his hammock for a nap.

"Come on," sighed
Pirate Nong.
"Let's find his pet,
then we can go home."

But as the pirates
stepped onto the gangplank
Noddypoll slipped . . .

9

and fell in the water.

"Help!" he screamed. "I can't swim!"

Suddenly, a huge toothy creature tossed
Noddypoll up in the air.

"Help!" he screamed. "I want my mum!"

Captain Pepper jumped
to his feet. "Bless my soul,
it's a hippopotamus!"
he shouted. "That
would make a good pet.
Bring it on board!"

The hippo didn't want
to be brought on board.
It snorted and stamped
and snapped at the
pirates.
But at last they
hauled it up
onto the deck.

"Welcome aboard, my hippo pet,"
said Captain Pepper.
"With you by my side, I'll soon be
famous all over the world."
He patted the hippo's head.

The hippo snorted . . .

and rushed across the ship.

CRUNCH!

It bit the mast in two.

CRASH!

The mast fell

onto the deck.

"Stop that now!" the Captain bellowed.

Captain Pepper glared at the hippo.

The hippo glared at Captain Pepper –

and charged!

Captain Pepper dived out of the way . . .

but the hippo kept going . . .

right over the side of the ship . . .

SPLASH!

"That hippo was trouble," said Pirate
Nong. "Can't we go home and buy
a parrot?"
Captain Pepper snorted and snarled.
"A parrot?" he roared. "Not on your
nelly! Find me something different,
or I'll feed you to the sharks!"

Chapter Three

The pirates set off into the jungle.

"The Captain should catch his own

pet," grumbled Noddypoll.

"Shhh!" said Nong.

"Look, by that tree! That's different."

A porcupine was scratching for grubs.

"It's black and white

like our pirate flag,"

said Nong.

"That would make a good pet for
Captain Pepper," said Noddypoll.
"Catch it, Noodle, before it runs off."
Noodle reached out his hand.

"Oww!" he squealed, and leapt in
the air. "Shiver me timbers!
It's covered in sharp things.
I'm not picking that up.
We'll find something else."
So on they went, tiptoeing slowly.

Suddenly, something hit Noddypoll on the head.

"Ouch!" he howled. "Who's throwing things?"

The pirates looked up into the trees.

The monkey threw another
nut, then it leapt to the
ground.
"That's different!" cried Nong.
"That would make a good
pet for Captain Pepper,"
said Noddypoll. "Catch it,
Noodle, before it runs off."

Noodle ran after the monkey, with
Noddypoll and Nong at his heels . . .

all the way back to the *Snooty Fox*.
"It's going on board!" said Noddypoll.

The pirates chased the monkey up the gangplank and onto the ship.

The monkey jumped on the Captain's hammock, and stole his hat.

Captain Pepper woke up from his nap.
"Stop!" he bellowed. "Give me back
my hat!"
The monkey climbed up the ropes
and swung on the sails.

"Get off my ship!" the Captain roared.

He waved his cutlass in the air.

SWISH! SWASH!

The monkey screeched and dropped the hat.
Then it ran down the gangplank and
disappeared back into the jungle.

"That monkey was trouble," said
Pirate Nong. "Can't we go home and
buy a parrot?"

Captain Pepper snorted and snarled.

"A parrot?" he roared. "Not on your nelly!
Find me something different, or I'll feed
you to the sharks!"

Chapter Four

It was getting dark when the pirates set off into the jungle again.

Noddypoll clung to Noodle and whimpered.

"Shhh!" said Nong. "Look, over there."

"A pussycat with spots! That's different," said Noddypoll.

"Catch it, Noodle, before it runs off."

"Here, Pussy," called Noodle.

"Come to Noodle, good Pussy."

The leopard crept
slowly towards him.

28

But the growl in its throat and the glint in its eye filled Noodle with fear.

"Shiver me timbers! He thinks I'm his dinner!" he cried.

Noodle turned and ran deeper into the jungle, with Noddypoll and Nong at his heels.

The jungle grew darker and even more scary.

On they went, tiptoeing slowly.

Then Noddypoll tripped over a fallen branch and landed on his bottom with a howl.

The branch began to wriggle.

"Aagh!" screamed Noddypoll.

"That branch is alive!"

"Well, shiver me timbers!" said Noodle.
"That's different!"

"Catch it, Noodle, before it runs off,"
said Noddypoll.

"It can't run," giggled Noodle.

"It's got no legs!"

He grabbed it by its middle and pulled.

"It's heavy," he cried. "You'll both

have to help."

Together, the pirates carried the snake through the jungle and back to the *Snooty Fox*.

Captain Pepper couldn't believe his eyes.
"A python! You've brought me
a python!" he cried.
He hopped and skipped across the deck.
"I'm going to be famous!" he whooped.

Then Captain Pepper clapped his hands
and began to sing:

"O, a python is a wondrous thing,

No arms, no legs has he.

And yet he moves with lightning speed

To catch and eat his tea."

"We've found you a pet," said Nong.

"Can we go home now, please?"

Captain Pepper stopped singing.

"Go home?" he roared. "Not on

your nelly! We're going round the

world to show off my python.

I'm going to be famous!"

The pirates grumbled behind his back.

"We'll be off at daybreak," said the

Captain. "So you'd better be ready,

or I'll feed you to the sharks!"

Chapter Five

Daybreak came.

The pirates slept peacefully in their bunks.

At midday, Nong woke up and stretched . . .

"Something isn't right," he thought.

"Hey, wake up Noddypoll and Noodle," he called. "It's late. Why hasn't the Captain shouted at us?" The pirates crept up on deck and tiptoed towards Captain Pepper's hammock.

There were the Captain's boots . . .

There was the Captain's hat . . .

but there was no sign of Captain Pepper.

In his place, fast asleep, was

Captain Pepper's python pet –

with a large bulge in its middle.

"Where's the Captain?" cried

Noddypoll.

The pirates stared at the sleeping snake.

"I think *that's* the Captain," whispered

Nong, pointing to the bulge in the

python's middle.

"Well, shiver me timbers!" said Noodle.

Then suddenly Nong began to cheer.

"Now there's no one to shout at us!"

he cried.

"There's no one to feed us to the sharks!"

shouted Noddypoll.

"There's no one to stop us going home!"

called Noodle.

The three pirates jumped for joy.

"First let's send Captain Pepper's pet back where it came from," said Nong. The pirates pulled back the hammock – HEAVE!

And let it go –

TWANNNNNG!

The python flew through the air –
WHEEE! – and back into the jungle.

"HOORAY!" shouted the pirates.
And they danced a merry dance all
round the deck.

Chapter Six

Noddypoll, Noodle and Nong sailed back across the sparkling seas until at last they arrived home.

The three pirates sold the *Snooty Fox* for a fortune, and bought a tea shop instead.

On a perch in the tea shop window sat a parrot, to welcome all the visitors.

As for Captain Pepper, his wish
came true.

He soon became famous all over
the world.

Captain Pepper was the only pirate
in history to have been swallowed
by his pet!

About the Author and Illustrator

Sally Grindley is an award-winning author, and pirates are some of her favourite characters. "I like writing about pirates because you can make them as silly as you like," she says. "And the crew in this story are definitely as silly as any I have ever met!" Sally Grindley's other books for Kingfisher include *The Giant Postman*, *What Are Friends For?*, *What Will I Do Without You?* and *Will You Forgive Me?*

David Parkins has illustrated lots of books for children, and is also the artist behind the *Beano*'s Dennis the Menace. "I love being an illustrator," he says, "but running a tea shop sounds fun, too. I'd find it difficult to resist all the cakes, though – especially the treacle tarts!"

Tips for Beginner Readers

1. Think about the cover and the title of the book. What do you think it will be about? While you are reading, think about what might happen next and why.

2. As you read, ask yourself if what you're reading makes sense. If it doesn't, try rereading or look at the pictures for clues.

3. If there is a word that you do not know, look carefully at the letters, sounds, and word parts that you do know. Blend the sounds to read the word. Is this a word you know? Does it make sense in the sentence?

4. Think about the characters, where the story takes place, and the problems the characters in the story faced. What are the important ideas in the beginning, middle and end of the story?

5. Ask yourself questions like:
Did you like the story?
Why or why not?
How did the author make it fun to read?
How well did you understand it?

Maybe you can understand the story better if you read it again!

About the Author and Illustrator

Sally Grindley is an award-winning author, and pirates are some of her favourite characters. "I like writing about pirates because you can make them as silly as you like," she says. "And the crew in this story are definitely as silly as any I have ever met!" Sally Grindley's other books for Kingfisher include *The Giant Postman*, *What Are Friends For?*, *What Will I Do Without You?* and *Will You Forgive Me?*

David Parkins has illustrated lots of books for children, and is also the artist behind the *Beano*'s Dennis the Menace. "I love being an illustrator," he says, "but running a tea shop sounds fun, too. I'd find it difficult to resist all the cakes, though - especially the treacle tarts!"

Tips for Beginner Readers

1. Think about the cover and the title of the book. What do you think it will be about? While you are reading, think about what might happen next and why.

2. As you read, ask yourself if what you're reading makes sense. If it doesn't, try rereading or look at the pictures for clues.

3. If there is a word that you do not know, look carefully at the letters, sounds, and word parts that you do know. Blend the sounds to read the word. Is this a word you know? Does it make sense in the sentence?

4. Think about the characters, where the story takes place, and the problems the characters in the story faced. What are the important ideas in the beginning, middle and end of the story?

5. Ask yourself questions like:
   Did you like the story?
   Why or why not?
   How did the author make it fun to read?
   How well did you understand it?

Maybe you can understand the story better if you read it again!